NO ROOM for a SNEEZE!

A folk tale retold by Robyn Supraner
Illustrated by Irene Trivas

Troll Associates

Library of Congress Cataloging in Publication Data

Supraner, Robyn.
    No room for a sneeze!

    Summary: Unhappy with their overcrowded house, a man
and his wife go to the Wise Man who gives them some
unusual advice.
    [1. Folklore]   I. Trivas, Irene, ill.   II. Title.
PZ8.1.S947   1986   398.2'1   85-14164
ISBN 0-8167-0656-5 (lib. bdg.)
ISBN 0-8167-0657-3 (pbk.)

10   9   8   7   6   5   4   3   2   1

NO ROOM for a SNEEZE!

Once, a long time ago, a man
lived with his wife and their
seven children. They lived in a
small village, on a small farm, in
a very small house. With them
lived a dog, three cats, and a
goldfish.

Sometimes it was peaceful and
quiet.

But most of the time it was not.

The dog chased the cats. The cats chased the goldfish. The children chased each other. And the man and his wife fussed and scolded from sunrise to sunset.

"What a calamity!" said the man to his wife. "These things wouldn't happen if our house was not so small."

"You are right," said the
woman. "Our house is too
small."

At last, the unhappy couple
complained to their friends.

"You must go to the Wise Man,"
they said. "He alone can help
you."

So the man and his wife climbed the hill to the house of the Wise Man. They stood before him and told their story.

"There is not room to turn
around," said the man. "I cannot
bend to tie my shoelace. If only
our house were bigger."

"So much noise," said the woman. "Such yapping. Such yammering. It is worse than a circus."

The Wise Man closed his eyes.
He listened. Then he asked one
simple question.
"Tell me, are there animals on
your farm?"

The man and his wife grew
puzzled. They had not climbed
the hill to speak of animals.
But the woman said, "We have
some hens and a rooster."
"And some ducks and a goose,"
said the man.

16

The Wise Man clapped his
hands. He tugged his beard.
He tapped the side of his nose.
Then he said, "Go home, my
friends, and take the ducks and
the goose and the hens and the
rooster into your house to live
with you."

The man and his wife couldn't believe their ears, but they did as the Wise Man said.

Now try to imagine the uproar.
Chickens squawking! The rooster
cock-a-doodling! Ducks
quacking! The goose honking!
Feathers flying! And don't forget
the children!

The noise! The clutter! Night
and day! Day and night! Things
were worse than ever!

The woman sent her husband
back to the Wise Man.

"Dear Wise Man," he wept,
"what can we do? Now the
house is so crowded there is not
room for a sneeze."

The Wise Man looked at his
fingers. He looked at his toes.
"Tell me more about your
farm," he said.
"There is a mule to pull the
wagon," said the man.

"Aha!" said the Wise Man,
jumping to his feet. "Go home
and take your mule in the house
to live with you."
"Where?" cried the poor man.
But the Wise Man waved his
hand. He would say no more.

"Are you crazy?" yelled the woman, when her husband led the mule into their house. She hurled a pink petunia at his head.
"Husband, have you lost your wits?"

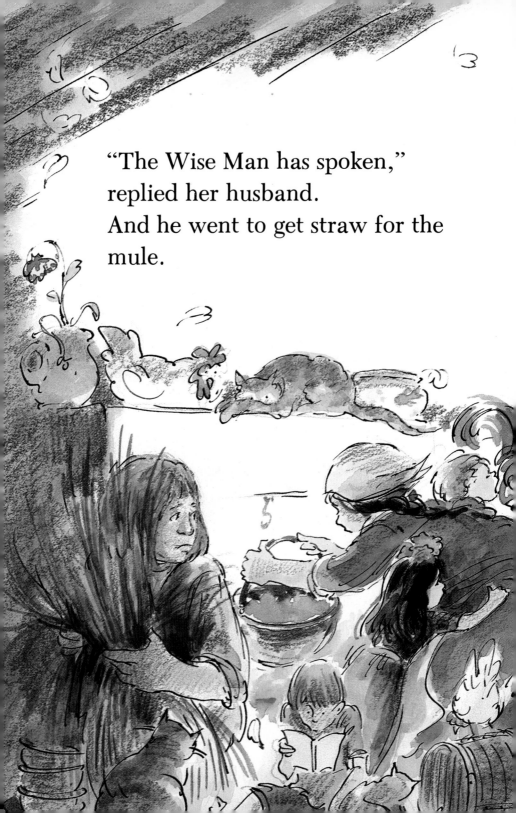

"The Wise Man has spoken,"
replied her husband.
And he went to get straw for the
mule.

The children rode the mule
around the kitchen. They dressed
it in their father's coat—and in
their mother's hat.

The husband ran back to the
Wise Man.

"Help me!" he cried. "My hair is
falling out! My wife will not
speak to me! Only a miracle can
save us!"

"Do you have a cow?" asked the
Wise Man.
The poor man nodded.
"Good," said the Wise Man.
"Bring her into the house to live
with you."

With tears rolling down his
cheeks, the man led the cow into
the house.

When the cow was milked, the dog upset the bucket. The woman sat on the hen's eggs. The mule broke the dishes. The children cried and squabbled. The man and his wife did not know what to do.

"Go back to the Wise Man,"
cried the woman. "Tell him he is
ruining our lives!"

"You are ruining our lives!" cried the husband. "You wouldn't believe what our house has become. The hens roost in my chair. The cow is eating the curtains. The noise! The smell! Do something!"

"There is a beggar in your village," said the Wise Man. "Invite him to come and live with you."

When the man came home with
the beggar, his wife almost
fainted. When supper was
served, the beggar ate it all. He
would not sleep on the floor with
the animals, but took the bed of
the husband and his wife.

The very next morning the husband ran back to the Wise Man. He held out his hands. He tried to talk but he could not.

"Things are terrible," said the
Wise Man.
The poor man mumbled, "Yes."
"You and your wife are
miserable," said the Wise Man.
"Yes," said the poor man. "Yes."
"I have found another home for
the beggar," said the Wise Man.
"Go home and tell him to leave."

The man ran home with the
good news. His wife packed a
lunch for the beggar. They
waved as he went down the
road.

That night the man and his wife
slept in their own bed. How very
good it felt.

The next day, when the goose
flew into the baby's cradle and
wouldn't come out, the man left
his house again.

He stood before the Wise Man.

"The time has come for the animals to return to the barn," said the Wise Man. "Go home now, my friend. Go in peace."

The man took the mule back to
the barn.

The woman led the cow away.

The children shooed the ducks
and hens and goose.

The rooster crowed and flapped
up to the roof.

Then the man and his wife cleaned and scrubbed and polished their little house. The children picked flowers and set them on the table.

"What a beautiful house we have," they said. "So quiet. So comfortable. So roomy."

Then, happily, they all sat down and had supper.